FOREVER CHRISTMAS
The Nativity

By

Thomas Weber

Illustrated By

Tamara Weber and John Kochansky

ISBN: 978-0-578-81576-3

Published in the United States of America

INTRODUCTION

In Forever Christmas, Thomas Weber takes a universal religious truth and weans a contemporary story of hope. You'll recognize all the characters. In fact, you already know them. Now, you'll understand them.

Rev. Alexander M. Santora

FROM THE AUTHOR

Ideas for this book came from observations of our entire family. Six daughters and a dog, ranging in age from twenty-two down to nine, each with a unique perspective on the world, religion and where we are heading as a people. In the end, I sat rethinking and rewriting, in an effort to bring hope and joy to a story for anyone who might read it. The words are mine, the ideas are general consensus over all age groups. While there is great reason for concern in our world, there is never reason to give up hope. Our human experience is ripe with inspirational stories of people triumphing over adversity.

I attempted to touch that little place in each of us that wants to say: "It could be worse", when at the moment, we really can't conceive of how.

Thomas Weber

CHAPTER ONE

December 14, 1993. Frigid, bone chilling winds tore at dying leaves clinging to bare tree limbs, overhanging the deserted pet dog play area in Washington Square Park, New York City.

Sarah trudged along, dragging her shopping cart and was nearly frostbitten. Having spent an extraordinary day, rummaging longer than usual, her cart overflowed with valuables garnered from the city's best trash piles, only available at this time of year.

It was getting late and she sensed a lessening of apprehension normally prevalent in the city air. Smiles brightened generally blank faces and music swirled continuously; vibrant voices raised in song, rather than anger. It was wonderful, intoxicating, but it wouldn't last. It never did. Chanukah would pass. Christmas would fade. She took full advantage of seasonal euphoria when collecting her treasures. Happy people dumped better junk and felt good about helping the less fortunate at this time of year. More often than not, room was needed in over-stuffed closets for new junk.

Scrooge would have held his own here, while Tiny Tim could not survive. Sarah didn't judge anyone. She had been rich once too, and now she was poor. It was matter of time and circumstance.

As a wealthy person, she was indifferent towards the less fortunate. Now she understood both sides. Poverty taught her that possessions were very important to people rich or poor and only unwanted items were easily discarded.

'Everyone should be poor and hungry for a day', she thought and continued on.

As darkness descended on the city, homeless everywhere were settling for the night and Sarah didn't intend to lose her warm spot in the PATH train station entrance. This would, undoubtedly, be the last night some would settle into a bitter cold sleep. They would disappear as if they never existed, and no one would mourn their passing. Many people said they deserved their fate to ease any guilt they themselves might feel. Of some, this might be true, but Sarah could not help thinking of the Tiny Tims among them.

Cast off treasures, gentle joyful creatures, unable to cope with life's trials, simply ignored to death. There is so little time to make our mark on the world. We don't take time to remove stains from our humanity, so why sweat the small ones? She sighed to herself, facing futility.

Night after night, hordes of nameless, faceless, forgotten people slept on street registers, coveting warmth rising from subway tunnels, in corners of elevators or abandoned cars. Sarah was headed for her place, hoping no one else had taken it.

Stopping briefly to get her bearings, she was drawn to a waif of a man sitting in the gutter on the corner of Eighth Avenue. Something compelled her to draw closer when all her street senses screamed: 'Stay Away! It's none of your darn business.' Strange, she mused but moved closer, throwing common sense and caution away unaware she could not have stopped had she wanted to. It was late, she was late, but she needed to soothe one troubled soul, or at least try to.

'Am I mad?', she questioned. 'It's Christmas,' she answered, feeling better because at Christmas, reason was suspended and anger ignored even on the streets of New York City.

The scrawny figure sat sobbing quietly, head resting on his forearm huddled in a fetal-like position against the cold. As she approached, she noticed a thin rubber surgical tubing around his wrist, hanging straight down. The shattered remains of a needle littered the ground between his feet and her instincts screamed again.

'Move on! You're being foolish.' But she didn't.

'Christmas spirit is like lunacy,' she laughed, exhilarated. This felt right, even if it was crazy. So, having little experience with strangers, she offered lamely:

"Merry Christmas, brother."

A starving child caught her eye on the television in a store window across the street, followed closely by an advertisement for a fifty thousand dollar car.

"The state of the world's mentality," she whispered, disgusted that she had placed more importance on the make of her car than the welfare of any child, hungry or not.

Poverty places priorities in perspective. She chuckled at her own alliteration. Sarah, once fabulously wealthy, hadn't appreciated it and now, due to poor investments and excess, was desperately poor. She had taken good fortune for granted. Life's cruel irony, she thought, her eyes glued to the small man huddled in the gutter.

He turned. His sunken smiling eyes stared out of dark blue circles and seemed somehow familiar, someone she should know. She felt no pity, only sadness at the waste of humanity in New York. The center of the free world.

He answered, "Merry Christmas to you too, Lady Sarah."

Sarah was startled.

"Roger?" She moved closer. "Is that…? Good Lord, what's happened to you? You look horrible."

"And I feel horrible, Sarah."

"Why? The last time I saw you was what, five years ago? You were introducing a new line of women's wear and a rising star in the glitzy world of fashion on Seventh Avenue. What happened?"

"The track was too fast and the flesh was weak. An old story. I got into trouble." He buried his face sobbing. "So much trouble, Sarah."

Still startled to see him, a part of her past, here in her new world, she asked quietly, as if afraid of his reply, "What trouble, Roger?"

"I've taken one needle too many and my beau will have me no longer. He threw me out."

"Why not stop, if you love him, Roger?"

"Doesn't matter now. Afraid I can't go back anyway."

"You have AIDS, don't you?" Sarah held her breath and he nodded. She felt helpless and sorry at the same time. "I'm sorry to hear it. What did Joseph say?"

"Joseph would live with the disease, but he hates drugs, Sarah. He always has."

"Joseph is gentle and kind, Roger."

"I know. And I am the fool of fools."

"It is a frightening disease."

"The plague to end all plagues, my love."

Indicating the broken needle her voice grew harsh. "And still you pour additional poison into your veins."

"No, I haven't, Sarah. I was going to, but I didn't and haven't for some time. Funny that now, having little reason to live, I find life precious. The thought of death is sobering and here, at its door, I'm finding a little peace for the first time in my life. Isn't that strange?"

"Not strange at all. We all cherish most what is in short supply", she said whimsically. "So you're on the streets now?"

"From the penthouse to the outhouse is not so far to fall."

"I know the trip well." She joked.

He laughed and nodded, a tear glistening down his cheek. "I'd forgotten. I'm sorry dear."

"Don't be, because I'm not. At least, not any longer. C'mon now. AIDS may or may not kill you, but if we don't hurry, the cold will kill us both sooner than I'd like."

Sarah reached down and lifted him to his feet. He had no strength to resist and instinctively drew near her for warmth. Two lost souls, two weeks before Christmas, clinging to each other for heat and comfort.

The coming of Christ always packs the stores, Sarah observed, searching for words, her mind spinning through their past lives while creating visions of life to come.

"Aren't you afraid to be with me?" Roger asked.

Sarah shrugged, "AIDS is all around us, hiding in bodies that haven't discovered it yet. We know you have it. Better the devil you know than the one you don't, Roger."

"You are incredible." He laughed then, the first time he had in weeks, and it felt good. Arm in arm they continued down 34th Street, passing shoppers who were more courteous than usual. Near the entrance of the PATH station on 33rd street they heard a bell ringing and a loud cheerful voice yelling, "Ho, Ho, Ho!" Rounding the corner, not ten steps from her nightly resting place, Santa Claus appeared in a frayed outfit, ringing his bell. He stood behind a tripod holding a tray full of change and dollar bills. Painfully thin, by Santa's standards, his tattered Salvation Army cape offered little resistance to the cold, but he seemed happy. They drew near and he called:

"Sarah Goldberg, is that you girl? A sight for sore eyes you are this cold evening. Merry Christmas, darlin'. I'd been hoping you were about."

She laughed in spite of herself. "Peter Daugherty, you old Irish devil you. Next you'll be asking what I want for Christmas. Does the Salvation army know you're representing them this year?"

"Ah, Sarah, as ever there was. The little I take in will last the winter and help a few others along the way."

"Help them how, to a few drops more wine?"

"No, girl, to food and water. I stopped drinking over a year ago. It's been that long since you gave me the boot, don't ya know. I've been working the streets for different reasons since. Actually I'm doing a little good, for once in me wretched life, girl. Wisdom came late and at a great expense, Sarah, but it arrived unscathed."

"Do you know how often you said that, Peter?"

"A thousand times ten, at least girl and then a thousand more again, Sarah. But without you around, I had to fend for meself, girl. I knew I would die and I nearly did, looking up from the gutter on more than several occasions." He chuckled.

Sarah laughed gently. "You never did care where you fell asleep when you were drunk. I got tired of picking you up."

"And rightly so, my love. I made love to that gutter more often than to you, and that's a shame on me, Sarah, but I've changed."

"I hope it's true, Peter. Now come on with us, we can all keep warm together for the night."

Peter didn't argue, having spent many nights huddled together with Sarah surviving the previous winters. He'd felt the piercing cold knife through him and he began wondering where he would spend the night. He was hoping she would be here, but had about given up when she rounded the corner.

Peter quickly folded the tripod, emptied the money into his sack and followed along. Roger clung to his surgical tube and Sarah's arm without speaking. Reaching the corner enclosed entrance to the PATH train, she gathered her treasures around them while Peter set up cardboard to block the wind. They settled for the evening. Sleep evaded them. Each sensed something unusual about to happen. They lay awake, waiting and wondering without uttering a word. Some time later, they realized each of them knew what the others were thinking. Entire sentences passed between them without a sound escaping their lips. The noises of the city faded and pleasant memories of three childhoods played in all their minds, simultaneously. They walked in each other's shoes, living each other's lives over, in a mere matter of moments. They came to realize how fragile each of them was and why. But more than this, they understood the frailty of all human kind. They experienced all of each other's joy, laughter and sorrow. Here at the edge of life and death they learned to care deeply for one another, and those around them, regardless of station.

Tonight, without knowing why, they were drawn to each other for more than warmth and comfort. They shared completely. These things were so simple, they had missed them in the hurry-up world. Reduced to the lowest level of their existence on earth, they found new life, or rebirth. The gift of love given with no expectation of a return and with no strings attached, inspired and filled their hearts. Here in the bowels of the city, a miracle was beginning.

A bright bubble of light settled, and surrounded them. There was no cold, wind or hunger within its scope. All of them stood simultaneously thinking, "Perhaps we've died."

They hadn't. They began gathering their things in the middle of the night without questioning why. It was time to go. For the very first time in their lives, it didn't matter where. Hope surged inside them.

A brand new blimp floated over the city with a strange message flashing brightly on its side. It circled slowly, then hovered, remaining almost directly above Sarah's resting place. It flashed and shed sparkling fireworks, enthralling them, especially the magical lights rolling around its skin. They sensed, more than read, the message and realized it was also the source of the mystical soft starlight surrounding them. Within it, there was no urgency or hunger. There were no needs. It was full of warmth, joy and comfort, like a mothers womb. Everything was unconfused, unhurried…certain. When the blimp moved slowly away, they followed without question. Many experienced the light, but chose not to follow along.

People were tempted, but no one was forced. They were busy shopping and socializing. They were always busy with something else more important, and no time to spare. Rushing, rushing, rushing to who knows where.

Sarah, Roger and Peter wished everyone would feel the calm, like a gull floating on gentle rolling ocean waves. Each grabbed important belongings only and moved through crowds of people who, for the most part, ignored them. Three homeless souls at peace, gaining knowledge with each step, feeling stronger and stronger. This was a special night. They carried gifts knowing it wasn't necessary. He only wanted them to come, because they were each more important to humanity than anything they might offer Him. He was coming back, as He had nearly two thousand years before. Only this time, He was going to make certain everyone knew they were welcome at His table. These three homeless souls believed, forming new ideas, experiencing new wisdom beyond imagination. Hope began to replace desperation.

The message flashing on the side of the blimp was clear to them, though few others understood. A band of beautiful lights formed no distinct words but conveyed a clear message. A paradox within a dilemma, until you looked with an open heart. Then, the message was simple:

from every

'Give each other a break, will ya? Stop judging each other so harshly. Come see the Messiah, before too long. He is appearing in Asbury Park. Don't miss Him. He offers love and peace of mind. Evil and hatred are going to get a beating tonight. You will find him lying in an abandoned building, wrapped in swaddling clothes, lying beside a manger, snuggled against a gentle dog. Come see.'

Sarah, Roger and Peter knew everyone would come to their senses. They had to. For now, they simply followed the light and understood the world desperately needed a miracle. They were part of it.

CHAPTER TWO

Joseph was angry, frightened and feeling lonely.

"I'm married. I'm only nineteen for God's sake." He complained to the walls and windows.

"Everyone knows this isn't my child. Yet Maria is wonderful. Why would she lie? After all this time. Why would she betray me?"

He loved Maria all his life and was hurt and hurting not knowing whom to trust or what to believe. He was trying to get it straight in his head when Levi, the weirdo, arrived in a yellow Volkswagen bug. He rolled down his window laughing.

"Joey, Joey, Joey! You're listening to your friends again and what's it got you? Confused. Worried. And why? I'll tell you why, son. You're worrying about what they'll think of you. You want to be accepted. Well, drum roll please, I'm here to accept you. I already like you, but more important persons than me have an eye on you, Joey. They expect big things. Very big things."

This hadn't done much to lift Joe's spirits, so the weirdo tried a different approach.

"Think about everything in your life that's true, Joey. Close your eyes now son and really concentrate. Your heart will answer you. The path before you is not easy, but most worthwhile things aren't. Maria told you what happened and your friends tell you what they think happened. See the difference?"

He didn't really, but that didn't slow this nut down. He was more enthusiastic than a lawyer at a train wreck. He continued.

"You decide what is true in your life. This is a very special night. God's love grows in your wife. She's done nothing wrong. You know it in your heart, but because of your friends' stupidity and jealous thoughts, you are having a hard time believing. Maria's child, your foster child, will prove once and for all, God exists. There will be no more questions. He brings peace for all time, to all daughters and sons, and you are chosen, buddy. How about that? Pretty neat, huh?"

Joseph just stared at him thinking, 'Why me, God?' But also realized, he is making sense. For a weirdo, that is.

The weirdo scratched his chin, eyed Joseph thoughtfully and continued. "Has Maria ever lied in all her life? Can you say the same for your friends? Has she ever hurt you or anyone else? How about your buddies, Joseph? Are you starting to get the picture? Jesus, Joey!"

Looking skyward, he spoke to the clouds, "Sorry, Boss."

His gaze returned to Joseph. "You are thick headed. Think, boy. You and Maria have been together since kindergarten. You slept in the same bed as children, told each other secrets and kept them safe. You've loved each other more years than most people remain married and you are only nineteen years old. You, a Jew, and she a Gentile. Who would have believed this possible two thousand years ago? I know I didn't, but I was younger then."

"What do you mean? How old are you?" Joseph asked.

"Thirty five hundred years old tomorrow. How do I look? Not bad, huh?"

"Not bad for a lunatic." Joseph answered under his breath.

Levi heard but pretended he didn't. "Hold her close in your heart, Joseph. Care for her. God sees your suffering and understands your confusion. Have faith and stand by Maria. Your blessings will fill endless hearts."

Joseph was feeling stupid and inadequate already. Now, this weirdo, claiming to be the Angel Levi, didn't seem so weird. He appeared to be a bunch of different people wrapped in one, changing appearance like a chameleon. What was worse, Levi made sense. Other people kept interfering with their happiness. They moved to Nazareth, Pennsylvania in hope of a change, a carpentry job and better luck. Things were better, but not much. Now they had to return to Asbury Park in order to vote, because they hadn't lived in Nazareth long enough to register. They traveled all the way to Bethlehem to argue their case, but it was no use. If they wanted to vote, they must return to Asbury Park. Making matters worse, none of Joseph's friends came to visit them because he married Maria. They called her dirty names and told Joseph he was being naive. He was angry with himself because they convinced him to blame her for their troubles and failed to defend her.

He cried bitter tears, knowing what his friends might say if he explained: 'Listen, guys, an Angel in a yellow Volkswagen told me Maria's having God's child. That's cool, right?' Yeah, sure. They'll believe that.'

Then he thought of Levi, asking himself; 'Who cares what my so called friends think, anyway?'

But it was a half hearted sentiment. The Angel / Weirdo, continually reminded him of Maria's goodness; their love and their trust for each other from infancy. Levi told him this was why they were chosen to care for God's child. Joe didn't know when he started crying, but tears flowed freely down his cheeks onto his shirt. "I'd be put away and never let out if I told them", Joey muttered to himself.

He kept thinking and thinking about all his friends cruelty and Maria's steadfast kindness and courage. Levi's words reverberated inside his head.

"Joey, Joey, Joey stop being confused. Open your heart."

All at once his breathing slowed, his mind cleared, and he understood. "God is here, when our world needs Him most. AIDS is killing us. Racism is killing us. Taxes are killing us. My friends don't understand Maria, or our love."

He was almost certain, as Levi explained in detail, there had only been one other like her in all the world's history, and that was two millennia ago. None of his friends believed he and Maria never slept together before marrying. Even after marriage, they only made love a couple of times, because Joseph was afraid, like any nineteen year old, of hurting the baby. It was easier just letting everyone believe the Child was theirs. Maria would have none of this lie. She was oblivious to ridicule. "An Angel came to me and gave me God's child to bear."

Joseph listened, thinking, "Everyone thinks she's nuts. I now how brave she is. Maria trusts her faith completely. She never complains."

He felt weak, especially when they mocked her and he avoided defending her.

Joe's family disowned them. His father didn't believe Maria's story about an

مصريا قتلوا في الخارج

Angel. He decided they were lying. The truth was difficult to deal with, even for a religious Jewish man waiting his entire life for the Messiah to make His first appearance. He closed the door in his son's face before Joe finished speaking. Joe's brother simply laughed at them. That's when they decided to move to Nazareth. Joseph never said it out loud, but he was bitterly disappointed in his family. Maria sensed his anger.

She smiled, patted her stomach and said, "Our family is here. Don't be angry at your Dad, Joseph. Put yourself in his place."

But he was angry, and worse, he questioned Maria's story in his own heart. Levi had almost convinced him, until now. On the way home, their car broke down. Everything seemed to be going wrong continuously.

Maria remained undaunted refusing to lose hope, but Joe continued to question.

She sat quietly, looking radiant and Joe thought, 'Just wait til He's born and performs a miracle or two.' He was still trying to convince himself when Maria came and stood by his side.

"Joseph, do you see that beautiful light over there? I feel so peaceful looking at it."

"Not now, Maria." He exclaimed.

She persisted. "But look at it Joseph. It is magical."

He refused again and Maria moved away. She knew he was hurt, but would eventually come to terms with it. God would see to it. She didn't feel like trying to convince him further.

Joseph chastised himself. "Fool" he whispered to himself, knowing Maria

was trying hard to touch his heart and he was being stubborn. He wanted to reach out to her. He wanted to hold her and trust God as she did, but his ego wouldn't let him. He watched her move away out of the corner of his eye. Even a pep talk from an Angel didn't dispel Joseph's doubts completely. Anyway, Levi seemed like a nut case, not an Angel. Against all this confusion, a seed was sown. It took root, and a miracle continued to grow.

CHAPTER THREE

Sarah, Roger and Peter followed the light from east to west, then north to south, and finally straight east towards the ocean. They paid for the PATH train to New Jersey and then walked. The blimp never moved very far in front of them. They never got cold, tired or hungry. They were happy, going along, convinced this journey was the most important of their lives. They were bringing gifts, making the trip for the sole purpose of offering themselves, as they had to each other. It was a nice feeling, the first for each of them in a long while. Some miracles are very small in the beginning, but have great possibilities.

Forty miles away, along Interstate Highway 195, Maria gazed at the light. She sat patiently waiting for help she knew would come, while her unemployed, carpenter husband, brooded over their misfortune. He spent hours watching cars whiz by without stopping. Now, darkness was falling like a curtain around them and Joseph began to despair. He was about to leave her to get help when a low slung, candy apple red '57 Chevy with chrome wheels swerved off the highway, crunched over the gravel and screeched to a stop next to them. Two dark skinned boys rode in front, while an olive skinned Mexican boy slouched in the back. The blast of speakers blaring music reverberated everywhere, causing the air to pulsate around them.

"What's up, homs?" The smaller of the two boys hollered from the passenger seat, while leaning out the window.

"Car broke down." Joseph raised his voice to be heard.

"No joke. That's tough. Wish we could help man, but that ain't our style. Merry Christmas Homeboy."

They sped away laughing and had not gone more than three hundred yards when a deer darted out in front of them. Swerving to avoid it, their car ran up an embankment and nearly flipped over. At the last second, just as they began to scream, thinking they might die, something unseen pushed the car back down and it settled at an awkward angle on the side of the hill. Joseph shook his head. He couldn't believe the car didn't flip. It was more than half way over when it settled back down. "Impossible," he thought, looking around as three frightened boys sat silently staring at each other inside the car, waiting for a death that didn't come.

Joseph caught a glimpse of a donkey painted on the trunk as the car flashed under the lights of the overpass. An image of the Blessed Mother, looking very familiar, riding an ass into Bethlehem filled his senses and he glanced back at Maria. The imagine, and Maria's face blended together, but Maria hadn't moved. "Weird", he thought. "This is all too weird." Levi leapt into his thoughts. He could hear him distinctly saying, "Nice save on the car don't you think, Joe?" Joseph looked all around, but Levi was nowhere to be seen. He still heard his voice. "This is all coming together now, Joe. Wait and see."

He moved to help the three wise guys just as the yellow Volkswagen appeared out of the darkness. Levi was at the wheel. He seemed different. Surreal,

Powerful, Intense and Angelic.

"You again?" Was all Joseph could say.

"Give me a minute with these guys, will you Joey?"

"They might be hurt. You may need my help."

"There you go again, Joe. O ye of little faith and all that stuff. Jesus, you are going to be the death of me." He glanced at the heavens. "Sorry, Boss. I know I'm never dead, but I love that saying."

Returning his gaze to Joseph, he added, "Trust me Joey. They'll be alright, okay? I didn't let the car flip did I?"

"It was you? I heard you, but couldn't see you."

"The old bug isn't as quick as it used to be, but I got here in time."

Then, speaking again to the air, "God. Some people are hard to convince. Are you sure about this guy? Sorry, Boss. Okay. Yeah, I'll see you later."

The deer, who forced them off the road trotted up and Levi spoke to him too. Joseph would swear later the deer had smiled.

"Did you just speak to him?" Joseph asked.

"Is the Pope Catholic? Does a Rabbi speak Hebrew? Do bears shi…" Levi stopped himself. "Forget that last phrase, and yes, I spoke to him, Who do you think summoned him in the first place? I thanked him, and explained these guys were behaving like jackasses, but weren't normally bad. He thought it was amusing and was happy to help. By the way, he ran in front of the car without being asked twice, Joe. No questions at all. He took it on faith alone. How about that, Joe? I also told him why Maria is special."

"You told a deer all that?"

Levi chuckled. "You question, even what you see with your own eyes. Thomas wasn't as hard to convince when we were here the last time, but he too needed proof, proof and more proof. Soon, you will believe you are never alone, Joey. We are never far away and your child is here to save a world He suffered for once before."

"Okay, Mr. Angel why don't I have a job? Why is my car junk? Christ did the poverty routine already. Why does his family have to be poor all the time?"

Levi sighed. "Lighten up, Joey. You're gonna have a stroke. Do you really believe you are suffering? You eat regularly and are warm. Not everyone in this world can say that."

"Huh, not tonight we're not, and we haven't eaten for two days."

Levi rubbed his chin, "There are children in your world who eat once a week and smile at their good fortune." Levi's patience was wearing thin. "You are God's instrument, son. In a world where people get high on drugs and mistake greed for happiness; in a world where having sex replaces making love; in a world where abortion is a form of birth control; in a world where people are starving, when America alone could feed everyone six times over; in a world where the suicide hotline is on an answering machine; in a world crying out for love, you are a part of the solution and you are getting to be a pain in my…"

He looked skyward, listening to the night wind. "I forgot. I'm sorry."

He turned back to Joseph. "He doesn't want us swearing, but you're really starting to piss me…". Thunder rolled in the heavens and lightning flashed stopping Levi in mid sentence. He wiped his brow, smiled up at the sky and began again.

"Try to imagine your blessings, Joseph. Love, in all its splendor is about to reach out through two innocent children who have loved each other forever. You are a vehicle and Maria is the bearer of hope. We will protect you, but you must have faith. At times, faith is all any of us has. These are the most important of times and the most difficult of times, because we choose to believe or give up hope. You were chosen because you and Maria love beyond human constraints, refusing to judge each other. Don't fail her now in this most special, yet difficult time, and don't fail yourself. You love as children do, unselfishly caring more for the other person. You were chosen for love, not any other innate talent or ability, just your capacity to love unfailingly, which is second only to Maria's."

Suddenly, Joseph thought he understood. He believed in his heart of hearts it could all be true. This was it: his one in a million. This was a lottery beyond money, the prize of prizes. The second coming of the Messiah. Joseph was filled with Christ's gentle spirit. Understanding allowed all his doubts and anger to fade away.

Levi chuckled. "About time", he said, stepping out of the car growing larger and larger before Joe's eyes. A brilliant light engulfed him. Joseph's eyes widened and Levi laughed. "I knew you'd see it our way. How do you like this? I only do it on very special occasions. It's a little like dressing up for the prom. Most times, I stick to the old VW and a pair or jeans." As he floated towards the boys' car, he spoke to Joseph over his shoulder, "I've been driving that bug so long, I almost forget I can do this stuff. I really enjoy showing off a little. Do you think the glow is too much?"

"No," Joseph stammered, "not at all."

As he finished speaking, choruses of song filled the clouds. Joseph looked up at Angels of every description, color, race and size filling the sky. Many types of beings Joe didn't recognize appeared, singing a combination of blues, country and rock. The clouds rolled with the beat. The three boys jumped from the car and fell to their knees shaking in fear. Joseph noticed a lamb tattooed to the olive skinned kid's hand and envisioned shepherds in their fields watching over their flocks,

"This is really lame." He whispered to himself. In the same instant he imagined Maria riding an ass into Bethlehem. She looked different, and it was a different time and place, but it was his love. Of this, he was certain. This vision was vivid, like a movie of the past playing in his mind of a time long before cars, roads and rock and roll existed. Yet the angels knew all the songs and more.

Levi touched each of the three boys and they stood up. Joseph knew what was expected of him and Maria. They were different than everyone else, not better, just different. Being different often meant being alone. These revelations were a little frightening and Maria touched his arm to settle his fears.

Levi floated apart from them, instructing the three young men to drive Maria and Joseph into Asbury Park. They were to find them shelter and keep them safe. He ordered them to keep watch, like good shepherds until the child was born. Then they should go out to tell everyone what they saw. It was time to come together, to place all differences aside. The choir of angels voices rose to a crescendo rivaling any concert ever heard.

Levi's voice deepened and boomed over it all, "God loves all of you. He is coming to reclaim his people from evil. It doesn't matter what you believe because He always believes in you."

As suddenly as it began, the concert ended. The light faded, and they were alone in the quiet, along the deserted highway.

The sudden silence seemed strange. Everyone looked at each other, wondering if it were all a dream, but Levi, still glowing faintly, set them straight before pulling away in his Volkswagen.

"I really enjoyed that. It's been awhile. Just remember, this is no joke, and no dream. It's the last chance, the last round up, the end of the line, so get it together. Love one another. It's very simple. Don't screw this up."

He pulled away while his shepherds, dressed like street kids, backed their cherry red 1957 Chevy down the hill. They hurried to collect Maria's and Joseph's things, and they headed into Asbury Park.

This miracle was about to spread like sand in a windstorm.

Maria and Joseph settled into the shepherds warm car.

Three wise people continued along the Garden State Parkway, surrounded by ghostly light. They were stopped several times by curious State Troopers who listened to their story and believed everything they were told, allowing the three to continue where no pedestrians were ever allowed. They were all going in the same direction.

CHAPTER FOUR

At that same moment, a little eleven year old street urchin huddled against a brick building in Asbury Park. He roamed the back alleys of the city, daily searching the best picking grounds. Smitty's Bakery for breakfast, the train station to shine shoes and hear a lesson from old Moses until lunch, then back to check on his animals and feed his charges. So it went through the day. He was what the academics of the world characterize as a survivor.

The Sun's warmth, embedded deeply in the brick during the day, oozed out slowly warming his back and shoulders. Erik had just finished feeding his flock of two small children, a dozen cats, three pigs and a blonde Labrador Retriever. He lives by his wits and has for several years. He knows no other way. On his own from such an early age, he thinks this is normal. While other eleven year old children were busy with homework or cookies and milk, Erik was rummaging inside a Salvation Army dump for warm clothes. He lived in one of those metal clothes deposits for the first year after his dad died from a drug overdose and his mom disappeared. His education came from old Moses, down at the train station. He followed along with Old Moses. (Erik thought Old was his first name.) Moses didn't mind. His old yellow Volkswagen sat parked outside and everyone he knew called it the Old Bug. Nicknames seemed pretty cool and 'what's in a name anyway?' He smiled to himself, while he cleaned the station rest rooms with Erik's help. Moses taught him to read and write. He told Erik stories and taught him to love music and people.

Erik trusted Old Moses, who could smile better than anyone, ever. His blue-black satin smooth skin glistened, especially in moonlight. Full lips stretched all the way up to the top of his gums, exposing snow white teeth matching his hair. When he smiled, it lit up the entire station. His eyes drew you in. Pain lived in those liquid, sapphire orbs; a little sadness, a vault of wisdom and an ocean of warmth that whispered, "Talk to me. Tell me your troubles. It isn't as bad as you think. I've seen it all. I will understand. Talk to me."

Erik recognized the old man's gift of understanding at once. Yes, he trusted Old Moses, but it was more than trust. Erik loved him and knew Old Moses loved him back. They never spoke it, but they knew. Erik talked and talked to Old Moses and Old Moses never cut him off.

After resting a few minutes against the brick wall, enjoying the crisp clear night, he rose, stretched and looked up into a purple black sky full of twinkling stars. A cold front passed through cleaning the air, making the night sky appear deeper and broader with no end to its silent majesty.

"It is infinite." Erik says and smiles, having just learned the word 'infinite' from Old Moses. He likes its feel in his mouth and was glad he could use it. "Infinite!" He said it again and laughed.

"Infinite means never ending. No beginning, no end, like a circle or God, if there was one up there." Old Moses insisted there was because without God, there wouldn't be flowers or the bitter sweet sound of the blues. But Erik wasn't quite convinced about anything he couldn't see. Kily Wong tugged at his coat and he glanced down at his little six year old friend. Her parents were killed a month before in a shooting at their convenience store. Killed because they didn't understand the thief's demands for money, of which they had very little anyway. Erik found them lying in their own blood with Kily sitting nearby waiting for them to wake up. He led her away before the police arrived. He didn't trust Social Services.

Now, she leaned against his leg and he pulled her close, but his gaze returned to the sky. A brilliant blue-white light radiated from a shiny object to the east. To the west, a huge yellow glow filled an entire section. Erik heard all kinds of music, mixing, drifting, and floating on the air. Light and music swelled, louder and louder like fireworks growing to a grand finale. Then it was gone: Vanished. Nothing, as if a plug were pulled on a lamp and the stereo simultaneously. He strained to see or hear. Nothing, but the rich blue-white beam in the east remained, appearing to move slowly towards him along with the overwhelming shroud of light to the west. He watched it for a while then went inside to play with Kily and check on John, who was ill. Thirty minutes later, he returned outside to discover he was right. The beautiful light was still moving towards them along with the shroud, which appeared to take on the shape of a large building made of light. An odd sense of ease filled him as he stood staring. The children settled to sleep with no arguments and Kily didn't toss and turn with bad dreams. Erik wondered if the light was affecting them somehow, then remembered they had heat and were warm. That was probably it. As he watched, he wasn't cold at all, though the temperature was in the teens and he hadn't put his coat back on.

He returned inside without so much as a shiver. He couldn't remember any of his worries and felt all was well. Touching the coat he had forgotten to put on, he checked on Kily and John. They slept on quietly for the first time in weeks. It is the way of children to trust implicitly. Childlike wonder itself is a miracle and we all love tales of miracles.

Now's the time
HOPE FOR THE FUTURE
Christmas Is

CHAPTER FIVE

J.J. Newberry's displayed a huge red and white banner:

'Open, every night-all night til Christmas.'

Erik lived in the storage barn behind the store, which once housed Asbury's famous Carousel. The brightly colored, hand painted horses, with flowing tails and long battle skirts were gone, sold off long ago to collectors. But figures of ducks, camels, goats, cows and all sorts of animals were still stored here. He ate the remains of dinner extracted from the Labrador Lounge and Piancone's garbage dumpsters after Kily and John were finished, in case they wanted more. They needed their strength this time of year, or they would battle recurring sickness all winter. Erik's immediate problem was flu. John, smitten by the bug early, was awful sick and required a doctor, which cost money. Erik racked his brain without a solution for two days. Tonight, watching that strange light in the sky, it came to him.

After covering Kily, wrapping John in old sheets and putting his plate away, he took out a worn pair of drum sticks, stuffed them in the back pocket of his jeans, reversed the baseball cap on his head and walked outside towards the main entrance of the store. Smoothly, displaying an economy of movement great musicians, artists and athletes all share, he turned over several old five gallon paint buckets and a couple of plastic containers. For cymbals, he added a garbage can lid and different pieces of tin. Lastly, he rolled in a old wash tub for his bass drum, took off a shoe and jammed a stick between his first and second toe, which protruded from a hole in his sock. He settled onto a wicker basket, tested tapping the bass drum and then with a silken rhythm, began. Slowly at first, feeling his way, warming up, letting the music flow inside his head. As he relaxed, his rhythm got better. He was good. Better than good. Erik was excellent. Old Moses taught him about music early on. Now it lived in him, like his soul, as if intended always for some special purpose. He could play several instruments and never had a lesson. He played all by ear, but drums were his favorite, Keeping the beat freed him, music freed him, allowing him to soar, flying over his drums, spinning, bouncing, hands and sticks a blur, smiling every second, enjoying every moment, savoring every sound. A crowd began to form. The manager of the store glanced out, saw who it was and returned inside. Erik was good for business. He flowed from drum to drum, hearing songs in his head, spinning his sticks in the air regularly, a born entertainer. Old Moses called him "The Little Drummer Boy." He knew someday soon he would play a great concert for someone very special. He could feel it. The crowd roared when he finished, and most went inside the store. It was the first time Erik noticed them. His little cardboard box over-flowed with change and bills. The store manager dropped in an additional ten dollars. "You're gonna hit it big someday kid." "Thanks Bill, I already did. Look at my box. It's enough for a doctor for John, don't you think?"

"If it's not, you tell him to see me, Erik."

"Thanks Bill, but you have your own family."

"I know, I know, but I can help a little." He smiles at this eleven year old little man thinking, 'If only he could get a break'. But it wasn't likely. There were a lot of talented people in the world and they have never made it. Bill went back inside shaking his head sadly. "He's a great little kid and so young, but not in the right place at the right time."

Little did he know that God was listening closely. He was listening to joy, sorrow, aspirations and broken dreams. He was listening to old hurts and little drummer boys. He was listening to Bill worrying about someone else's child and it was music to His ears. Of all the room in the universe, this was the right place at the best of time.

CHAPTER SIX

Lenny didn't worry about cars lining the sides of the street preventing him from parking. He turned up Bond Street and in the middle of the block two orange safety cones came into view. He ran over them pulling into a parking place at the curb.

Joseph asked, "Shouldn't we park in a different spot?"

Mario answered, "This is our spot."

"But the cones?" Joseph questioned.

"We put them there, homey. To save the spot. Smart, huh?"

Joseph began to protest, but Maria, on the verge of laughter, silenced him with a touch.

Lenny asked another question. "Who was the guy in the Volkswagen, Maria?"

"He told you who he was, Lenny."

"He's really an Angel?"

Maria nodded. "You three tough guys were chosen by God Himself. He sent you, His messenger, and a chorus of angels, and a deer saved your lives. What more proof do you want?"

"Jesus!" Lenny exclaimed.

"You shall have Him too." Maria added, patting her stomach. "And sooner than we thought, I'm afraid."

Joseph's eyes widened, but Maria's meaning was lost on Lenny, who was busy explaining his poor choice of words.

"No, I didn't mean Jesus the person, I meant, holy cow or something. I was surprised is all. I ah, forget it…"

"Maria knows what you meant, Lenny."

"There is one thing though Maria." Mario broke in.

"What is it?"

"We was wondering if God is..If God is..ah"

"If God is what, Mario?" Maria questioned gently. Mario became flustered under Maria's intense stare.

"Oh, Christ, I don't know. We're used to swearing all the time and the Angel shows up and saves our butts. Damn, we're used to swearing all the time, Maria."

"See! It's hard not to use swear words, Mario." Lenny interrupted. "What we're getting at, ah, damn, Maria, we want to know if God is black, white or Mexican."

"Yes, He is," Maria answered, eyes sparkling, trying to hide her amusement at their intensity.

"He is what?"

"He is what you asked, Lenny."

"C'mon Maria. You're pregnant with His child, you must know what race God is."

Maria frowned and asked, "If He is White, Jewish, or Protestant, or Asian, won't you love Him?"

"We didn't say that."

"Good, because that would upset Levi. You don't want to upset Levi again do you?"

They answered in unison. "No way."

"It's like this guys: God expects you to love everyone, no exceptions: Black, White, Jew, Muslim, Cross-Eyed, Crippled, you get it? Everyone."

"I knew it, Mario," Lenny stated. "God's white." It's our penance, our personal hell. We wind up working for whitey. Maria's trying to let us down easy. I told you we shouldn't cut school today, but no, you needed a ride in the country."

Levi came putt-putting around the corner in his yellow bug. "You three are really beginning to annoy me, and I went out on a limb for you with the big Boss. I thought I made myself clear and you understood. It is very simple. Keep watch till the child is born and safe. It doesn't matter what race He is. His love is for all. His forgiveness knows no bounds. His wisdom is beyond your understanding. You are chosen. Keep watch. Keep Maria and Joseph safe. Stop questioning and do as I asked or I will be forced to kick your sorry…"

Gazing skyward, "I know, I know. Sorry, Boss."

He returned his attention, back to the kids. "If you want to be replaced, tell me now." Levi's voice boomed like thunder through the neighborhood, reverberating off walls, through houses, into their souls, yet he barely opened his mouth.

All three hung their heads, "No, please, Mr. Angel Levi. We will stop complaining.”

"Good, because Lenny's real dad is Hindu. Now look at me." They looked up. "What race am I?"

Lenny shook his head, "My dad is Hindu."

They all looked at Levi. Their jaws dropped in unison. They couldn't tell. Levi changed and his beauty was overwhelming. There was no way of knowing his particular race. There were tell-tale signs of several cultures, but no definitive factor. He was part of all cultures.

"Well, I'm waiting." the Angel beckoned.

Lenny summoned his voice, "We, ah, we aren't sure."

"Yet, you obey me and I'm telling you the One who comes tonight is far greater than I."

Mario chimed in, "We're real sorry, Angel man. We won't forget again."

"Good." Levi's voice softened, lessening, losing its fury, becoming satin smooth. "From now on, ask the Child your questions and don't assume anything about Him. Remember, He is for all of us. That includes me and my own short comings. For now, keep your faith."

Lenny still shook his head "My dad is Hindu."

Levi glared. All three bowed their heads and nodded.

"Oh, one more thing." Levi's voice rose again.

"Anything, bro." Three young voices came in unison.

"Return the cones to the Highway Department." Levi winked at Joseph and Maria.

She smiled. Joseph laughed as Levi drove away.

Mario and Lenny hurried after him scouring the city for places to stay, but there were no rooms to be found. Every Motel and Inn was booked for the big Christmas concert at Convention Hall this weekend. Red neon 'No Vacancy' signs hung everywhere. They returned with the bad news, disappointed because they failed and were surprised when Joseph and Maria thanked them for trying so hard. Maria assured them something would turn up, giving Lenny an idea. He wandered over towards the crowd gathered in front of Newberry's just as Erik was finishing up his impromptu concert.

"What's up, Erik?"

"Same old, same old, Lenny. What's up with you?"

"Not much man, unless you consider meeting an Angel and being chosen by God, much, and finding out I might be Hindu."

"No kidding, say hello to God for me will you, bro?"

"I'm serious, man. I met an Angel who says God's Son will be born again, possibly tonight."

"Christmas isn't for a couple of weeks, Lenny."

"That was the first time, Erik. This is the second one. You know the one everyone calls the second coming at the end of the world? Anyway, none of that fire and brimstone stuff is what it's about. He is going to make things better for everyone. Isn't that fresh? I'm telling you He might be born tonight, only…"

"Only what, Lenny?"

"Only we can't find them a place to stay, man."

"Duh, Lenny. No room at the inn, huh? You're kidding, right?"

"No joke, Erik. Do you have room in the old store room for a couple more people to stay the night?" There's no room anywhere else."

"How many? You're sure they won't hurt the kids or the animals? They aren't weirdos or drug freaks, are they?"

"No way, homey I told you who they are. We dumped on them and they forgave us."

"Okay, no worries man. Bring them over."

"We have heat too, Lenny," Erik answered, thinking this is one of the best stories Lenny every came up with. "You guys are welcome to stay too."

"Heat? How come?"

"Newberry's is open every night until Christmas now. Who are these people you met?"

"I told you, God's mother and stepfather."

"Lenny, first you tell me you met an Angel. Then you need a place for God's mother to stay because there is no room at any motels."

"I know it sounds crazy, but wait until you meet Maria."

Her husband's name wouldn't be Joseph, would it man?"

"How'd you know?"

"Just a wild guess. Bring everyone back. There's more than enough room and I'll go to the 7-11 and get some food."

"Thanks, Erik."

"Thank you, Lenny. I never thought I'd meet God before I was twelve."

"It's no joke, Erik. I know what you think, but I'm not lying."

"Get everyone settled, Lenny." Erik usually dismissed everything Lenny said, but he was tempted to believe him this time. Yet, that wasn't quite right.

Erik didn't want to believe Lenny, but he did believe him, which was altogether crazy because Lenny always lied.

"Thanks again, Erik."

"You're welcome." Erik called over his shoulder, thinking; "what the heck, it's Christmas. I'll probably come back to a couple of strung out freaks, carrying signs like: Repent, the end is at hand. Or, God will destroy the world on June 4."

Lenny just waved at him and repeated, "Wait til you meet Maria. I promise you won't be sorry."

Erik headed for the 7-11 on Main Street. He planned on feeding everyone including the dog and still having enough to take John to the doctor.

Old Moses, his janitor friend, believed in a loving God, who allowed people to do what they wished. He explained to Erik that humans placed restrictions on God to fulfill their own selfish needs either for money or power, not the other way around. Erik liked that lesson. It explained much of the hatred Erik saw around him. The lesson freed his heart from believing in a vengeful God. Rather, Old Moses taught him of hopeful, joyful beliefs and expectations, while believing in an understanding, merciful God. A God who would allow him to enjoy the ocean, flowers and cartoons, which he watched in Newberry's window every day without feeling guilty all the time. Still, he harbored doubts about God's existence and Christianity. Turning the other cheek was okay when nobody was standing behind you with a gun. He had said as much to Old Moses and his friend had laughed.

"I guess I'll have to sleep on that one, boy," was his reply and Erik felt good because Old Moses had laughed.

When he returned to the storage room with multiple bags of food, Maria was in the first stages of labor. Her face aglow, she smiled at him through her discomfort. Joy filled her sparkling eyes. Maria's velvety light brown skin glistened with perspiration. Erik dropped his packages as much from shock as awe.

"Lenny told me the truth," he whispered.

Joseph spoke to him quietly, "Lenny told us you doubted his story. It's probably the first time he's told the whole truth in his life."

Joseph's voice was warm, kind and certain. His doubts were gone. "Child, you've done no wrong," he explained. "Watch with us for the world's Messiah. I needed a lot more convincing than you."

"What can I do for Him, Joseph?"

Joseph chuckled, examining the food Erik brought. He waved his hand indicating the shelter, the children, and the animals Erik took in and said, "I think you've done enough, my little friend. You have provided more for your family than I could for mine."

His voice held no malice or guilt. Joseph accepted his blessings as they came and glancing at Mario and Lenny he added with a chuckle, "And from whoever they come." He didn't want to dampen the child's enthusiasm and noticed drum sticks stuffed in Erik's back pocket.

"When our Child is born, Erik, will you play your drums for Him?"

"Hell, yes!" Erik exclaimed loudly.

Joseph flinched, startled by Erik's overenthusiastic response and Erik explained. "Sorry, I didn't mean to curse, but this is it, Joseph. This is my big chance. I had this feeling, you know? Each time I play my drums, I get better and better and I just knew there was a reason. I knew I was intended to play for someone special. I just didn't know how special. I thought it was just a dream, but it wasn't. The feeling was real. Old Moses told me, but I didn't want to hope too much, Joseph. I didn't let myself need it. It was a dream, and as long as it was a dream, I could keep it, you know. No one could take it away from me. This is moment I've been waiting for."

Joseph settled his arm around Erik's shoulder. "It's all that and more. It is the moment the whole world has watched and waited for, Erik. This is the return of God's son, or the Messiah."

"Moses explained that to me and I didn't believe it, but it doesn't matter. I'll play for Him, Joseph. I'll play my best for him. Everyone in Asbury will come. I will play the best I've ever played, Joseph. I promise I will. You'll see."

Maria spoke, "That's a wonderful gift, Erik." She grimaced as another contraction took hold, adding, "And you don't have long to wait."

Erik noticed John sitting quietly, listening and rushed over to him. His beautiful round, pink face was perfectly dry. Erik reached and felt his cheek. It was cool. John's fever was gone.

Normally, John would shove Erik away, claiming he could take care of himself. Not tonight. The storm raging inside him was over. He was at peace, almost happy. The feelings stolen from this tiny child were back. What had been erased by rage and fear born of uncertainty was returned. Erik found him abandoned, half frozen, sleeping in a car the previous year.

"How do you feel, little brother?"

"Good, man. I feel real good."

"When did you start to feel better?"

"I stopped sweating when that lady walked in, man. It was weird. She looked at me and smiled and I just felt real good, you know? One minute I was hot and sick and the next…"

"Do you know what's happening, Johnny?"

"I heard Lenny talking, Erik, but I didn't pay him no mind. You know the trash he is always talkin', but then this happens. They're here to start Christmas over again, man."

"Something like that, Johnny."

"That's fresh, Erik. A little scary, you know, but that's the freshest yet. Can I ask you something?"

"Shoot."

"Is this the end, or the beginning, man?"

"I don't know. I think it's a beginning. I sure hope it is, Johnny. He came to save us the first time, and I know He's big on forgiveness, but I don't think He's going to be real happy with what's been going on around here, if you catch my drift. We'll just have to chill and scope it out, buddy."

"What about you, Kily and me, Erik? I'm a little scared, you know. I done some bad giz, man. Do we get to be a family?"

"He loves you, Johnny. He cured you straight away, didn't He? Saved you from getting a shot from the doctor. Saved us a bunch of money. Must mean He likes you a lot. Maybe He will like all of us."

"You think so, man?"

"Yeah, I think so."

"Thanks, Erik. And, Erik?"

"What, John?"

"You think they have rappers in heaven, man?"

"God, I hope not."

Johnny smiled wide. "I hope they don't have no Roy Orbison or Eric Clapton, neither."

Erik laughed. "With our luck, dude, they'll be playing doctor's office music."

Joseph overheard. "Maria likes all kinds of music. We just heard a concert about two hours ago and there are sounds which will amaze you."

Johnny asked, "Was there any head bangers, man?"

Joseph was confused and turned to Maria who answered, "You won't be disappointed, little one." Johnny never spoke to anyone and Erik was surprised when he responded.

"That's fresh, lady. Thanks for making me feel better."

Maria patted her stomach. "It was our pleasure."

Erik slipped outside to his drums and began to tap them lightly, staring up in the sky at the blimp shining in the east. It was very close now. He could make out words running around the outside skin. He knew the message without reading it. He was thankful there was food and warmth for everyone.

After awhile, a few musicians gathered. One had an alto saxophone. His name was Big Tony and Erik invited him to join in. Sal arrived with an electric keyboard and his friend Cassie brought a twelve string acoustical guitar. Nancy showed up last with a bass guitar and they began to jam. Erik held up his hand and they paused. He rose and spoke to the crowd. As he warmed to his subject, everyone grew quiet. It was as if they were all waiting for an explanation, from an eleven year old boy.

Erik began, "Some of you won't believe what I'm about to tell you and that's too bad because the world has waited a long time for this night. God loves all of us, just as we are, and that's a miracle, if you ask me."

There was a little nervous laughter and murmuring then. People spoke in hushed tones until Erick held up his hand and the crowd fell silent.

He told them the entire story and when he finished, he sat down. The silence lingered without tension. The crowd waited patiently in expectation until this makeshift band eased into a soft, sweet rendition of Silent Night.

A strange sight they were: Sal the biker; Big Tony with enough dreadlocks stuffed under his wool hat to make it look like a giant mushroom; Nancy with orange, purple and blue hair; Cassie in neatly pressed jeans with a matching jacket; and Erik, playing Silent Night together, while the entire crowd raised their voices in song. Everyone gave their best, reaching out to one another, holding hands, feeling good for no apparent reason.

It was an awesome sight. Traffic snarled to a halt, but no one complained. No one robbed a liquor store, or shot anyone. Beautiful, musical strains drifted up and outward reaching beyond the city, to a blimp moving steadily nearer. leading three wise people. Examples of all human frailty and strength, seeking their Savior, bringing gifts of broken dreams, soiled spirits and desperation. The Messiah was ready for it all. It was time to make it all better. It was time to begin again. It was time for miracles.

CHAPTER SEVEN

Sarah dragged her cart straight up the middle of Main Street weaving in and out between cars stopped in the road. The streets were full of people singing. Everyone in the entire city joined in like some old time revival meeting. Roger sang along quietly while Peter sang out loud ringing his bell, and wishing people Merry Christmas. The guiding light continued past the musical gathering around Newberry's, stopping above a converted storage room at the edge of the ocean. Sarah hurried inside thinking, 'What a glorious season. What a wonderful feeling.'

The end of our war torn world arrived easily with no fire and brimstone. The special magical, mystical Christmas spirit arrived to stay forever on December 14, 1993.

Johnny and Kily sat at the rear of the storeroom. They watched in wonder with several cats, a pig and two goats, surrounded by crates of cleaning products and garden tools. In the center, lying on the floor, supported by dozens of old flattened cardboard boxes softened by sheets of plastic bulbs and crinkled newspaper, Maria, more lovely than light, rested entwined in Joseph's arms. She didn't stir, but was wide awake taking in everything at once. A tiny baby boy lay near her side, wrapped in swaddling clothes on top of a broken toy manger.

Luke, Erik's Labrador Retriever, cuddled himself around the baby keeping him warm. Three teenagers raced past Sarah and piled into a car with a Donkey's picture on the back. They were dressed in clothes that shepherds wore centuries before.

Roger watched them thinking, 'they must be in a Christmas pageant.' He was startled when he looked down and realized his own tattered clothes had turned to satin with a gold silk sash keeping his robe closed.

Lenny's red '57 Chevy turned into a cart and the donkey came to life to pull it. The three shepherds remained undaunted. After everything they witnessed this night, a car turning into a cart didn't surprise them at all. They knew God could do anything.

"He is the freshest, yet."

They told everyone they met, "Alleluia, God's Son is here, man, swear to God. He's here and you better pay attention 'cause He ain't fooling around this time. You better watch out and you better not cry 'cause all he wants is to love us and have us love each other. That's it, man. Get it done tonight. Love one another."

They repeated this news over and over without stopping or growing tired. They were doing God's work, a new set of the strangest apostles ever, the last the world would ever need.

Levi watched them from afar smiling, knowing God was pleased with his choice after all. Erik slid behind the drums and Big Tony and the others joined him in playing 'The Little Drummer Boy.' They could hear, but not see Levi or Old Moses singing the words. Tears streamed down his face as he turned back into the parking lot of the train station and put away the keys to his yellow Volkswagen for the last time. He strolled inside, took up his mop and pail and started cleaning the floor. His blue black satin skin shone in the moonlight and his liquid eyes conveyed an ocean of hope and compassion. He would miss teaching his little friend. He would miss being human with all the trials and uncertainties. He had been called many things over the centuries and had endured much evil. His reward was to see evil and hatred defeated at last and it was a great reward. He pushed the mop back and forth slowly as Erik's band played and the town sang. He hummed softly as they switched back to the strains of Silent Night thinking, 'this would have made a hell of a blues tune.' He chuckled and looked skyward, "Sorry, Boss, but I so love the Blues". He continued humming,

Sarah approached the Child wondering at the range of emotions she felt. Maria didn't speak, but nodded towards the manger and Sarah drew nearer. She leaned closer, close enough to smell the sweet baby smell and feel the child's breath. All her anxiety disappeared. She silently thanked Him. She lay all her treasures beside Him and left her cart. Sarah knew no one would ever want for anything ever again. The struggle of humanity to survive was over.

Roger came close, showed the Baby his clean arms and lay the surgical tube at His feet. The infant touched it, transforming it into a snake, which shriveled up immediately and died. The dark spots under Roger's eyes disappeared and his frame filled out. Roger viewed his body, felt the surge of vitality and was no longer afraid. God loved all His children, and Roger was His child. He had forgotten.

His love is infinite. It encompasses everything, and everyone. He moved away feeling a zest for life he had abandoned to a difficult lifestyle and to AIDS. He'd forgotten Christ was different also, a rebel, a feminist two thousand years early, an outcast from society who wouldn't accept hate.

The Savior is for all who love each other. He reflected and remembered how his own Joseph loved him, receiving nothing in return for so long, but willing to give more and more. At long last, he understood the strength of love given freely with no expectations. He reached for Peter and hugged him as a brother.

"Roger, boy in the heat of the night, the saints have gathered, son. You look marvelous."

Roger laughed hard from the pit of his stomach, "And I feel incredible. He loves us more than you or I could ever imagine. Go ahead, Peter. He is waiting for you." Roger moved outside only to find his own Joseph waiting.

Peter entered and draping his old tattered Salvation Army cape around the Babe, he whispered, "As ever there was, my Lord. This is a night of nights and you are the King of Kings." He was certain he was part of a miracle. The journey begun the day of Christ's death so long ago was at an end. This was home. The Messiah lay before him. It didn't matter if he was saved or not because he knew in his heart, evil was at an end. His personal demons didn't matter. This was reward enough. Peter decided to ask for nothing. Maria looked up at him with love in her eyes and spoke for the first time.

"Peter, you have suffered so much in war and in peace for what you witnessed in war. You have killed and watched children die in the name of honor. You saved more young lives than you took and through it all you hoped for an ending to all war and something better to come. You have your gift. There will be no more war. Forgive yourself now, Peter. That better time is at hand. Go with a gentle heart, because my Son loves you as well as any that has ever lived."

And Peter believed. He was as important as Moses, David or Solomon. He understood everyone was equal in God's eyes. This was the end and the beginning of life. The closing of the circle. All hatred and evil would be banished from the world, and he was among the first to feel God's love.

The Infant spoke into each of their hearts, healing their soiled spirits and sending them away with brand new dreams, never again to face desperation alone. They returned to New York by a different route. Each of them was astounded by their ability to speak and understand any language. They had no trouble convincing everyone they met that salvation and rebirth was at hand.

All around, the landscape was changing by the sheer strength of God's will. Garbage rotting in the gutters was disappearing. Old dilapidated buildings were restored to their original beauty. Miracles were commonplace. Normally poorly lit, dangerous streets were clear of hoodlums and freezing cold no longer existed. Man's mistakes were at an end because Christ did not intend to suffer again. The three wise people returned to a city restored. The City they left behind was transformed. No one was in a hurry. There were a few arguments going on, but with laughter instead of fury. All this occurred in just one evening. Nothing could stop the miracle of love once it began to spread.

CHAPTER EIGHT

At Newberry's the crowd carried Erik's makeshift drums to the stable and set them up. Tony, Sal, Nancy and Cassie slid in and tuned their instruments. Everyone pressed close around without shoving or fighting. The light from the blimp encompassed everyone. The air was electric with anticipation of something very special.

Erik settled and counted, two, three, four and started to play but the others didn't join in. He looked up and waited. Tony, Nancy, Sal and Cassie were leaving their instruments as others arrived. First, John Lennon sat in and sang "Imagine" with Janis Joplin. Then, Patsy Cline sang a gospel song with Otis Redding. Eric Clapton was in the crowd and his little boy arrived holding Martin Luther King Jr.'s hand. One by one they came, and Erik wasn't surprised or impressed. He had seen the Savior of the world and it didn't get any better.

Ghandi arrived chatting with David, Muhammad and Confucius. Bobby Kennedy and John came. Finally, carrying a bushel of fish and several loaves of bread followed by a large number of children, Harry Chapin came arm in arm with Old Moses, who touched Erik's face gently, still holding his mop, pail and a section of stone tablet given to him centuries before. Harry's inexplicable smile was still in place. They stood next to Erik. All together, the famous and the average. The great and the small. The rich and the poor. All joined in a rousing rendition of Amazing Grace.

The Child touched the little drummer's hand. The miracle was complete.

It didn't matter that Christ was Indian. It didn't matter that Christ was a Black man. It didn't matter that Christ was a White Man. He began as a Jewish child, who loves everyone. This is His gift and His best miracle.

EPILOGUE

There wasn't a hungry soul, a homeless mother, not so much as an unkind word spoken around the world that special night in December 1993, which marked the end of human frailty. Death was swallowed up by the presence of God. Fear, Greed, Lust, in fact, every painful and hateful trait learned by humanity began to disappear.

December 14, 3983: Gentle breezes slide silently through trees, barely pressing leaves aside in branches overhanging the pet dog play area in Washington Square Park. Nearly two thousand years have passed since God's Son returned and once upon a time, we did well. We found our greatest assets in each other and our greatest joy. We helped each other out.

Once a year, an ancient blimp circles the globe, signaling a festival. Angels fill the sky singing. Shepherds stand in fields, wise people everywhere thank God for a peaceful world. A Little Drummer Boy in Asbury Park, New Jersey, Sydney, Australia, Hong Kong, Taiwan and all across the world belts out a drum solo unequaled in history. It is a single night to rejoice and be glad that a Spirit of Joy exists three hundred and sixty five days a year. Humans no longer require special days or specific reasons to care for each other.

In the words of three young shepherds, riding around on a candy apple red Cart:

"Yeah, it's as simple as that man. You better watch out, 'cause He's serious bro. Ya gotta love each other, and for God's sake, don't cry unless they're tears of joy. Look at us. We been following His rules for two thousand years. We been straight a long time, homey. That's kicking man. Or, for you older folks, it's groovy. Ya know?"

THE END

P.S. Merry Christmas and God Bless because we believe and wish you well, every person of every creed and culture, every moment of your life.